JUNE *the* SWEET PRUNE

JUNE ETIENNE

My Dedication

I dedicate June the Sweet Prune to my Grandfather Alfred Vendor. I remember when he came home from work with a big bag of bread and sweet bread. I could not wait to get my hands on that hot bread. He also makes hot coffee for me, my sister and niece. It was fun growing up in grandfather's house every evening waiting for bread and coffee. Always take us to the movies, to my grandpa, I will always remember the good old days. miss you grandpa.

June the Sweet Prune
©2022 June Etienne

All rights reserved. This book or any portion thereof may not be reproduced or used in any manner whatsoever without the express written permission of the publisher except for the use of brief quotations in a book review.

print ISBN: 978-1-66788-400-4
ebook ISBN: 978-1-66788-401-1

CONTENTS

TATTOO	1
TRINIDAD	2
MY DAUGHTER AND SON	3
TRAVELING	4
DON'T COOK	6
WENT TO EMERGENCY ROOM	7
SURGERY	8
WINE	9
MOTHER	11
MORNING	12
MY DOG	13
LUNA	15
GINNY	16
MY SON & HIS FIANCÉE	17
STAY IN MY BED LATE	18
MY SWEET PRUNE GRANDCHILDREN	20

TATTOO

How I got the name JUNE the SWEET PRUNE it come from one special person at my work she calls me June the sweet prune and when I turn fifty, I got a tattoo on my Birthday no one believe I did it. They were touching it and I said this is what I always wanted to do when I turned fifty and I finally did it. Some of my family members have tattoos, my father, my son, grandson and brother. I like it and I would like to have one more. I'm just afraid of the pain. I admire people who have a lot of tattoos it's looks so beautiful how they do it I don't know. My son tattoo is gifted, lives life and one of me and his father. I will get my next tattoo soon on my back and I would like to take my daughter with me. She must get one with her mother. Getting a tattoo is a beautiful thing with friends and family. Christmas is the best time for my tattoo party can't wait for the party. I'm going to have a lot of food and drinks. People spend eight hours getting tattoos. My grandson has tattoos all over his body. I would love to have more tattoos, but I am afraid of the pain. At my Christmas party I will be brave and do some more.

TRINIDAD

I left Trinidad over 30 years ago. I went back about three times and the last time I was there was 17 years ago. Unfortunately, my dad passed away on valentine's day from covid it was hard and sad, but he lives a good life he was ninety-one. The sun was not genuinely nice to me, I had to wear a hat most of the time that I spent in Trinidad, but the food was amazing. I wish I had more time to go visit the beach.

Everything was strange and different. I also met some of my old friends and even my ex-boyfriend. t was happy to see everyone. My Father Funeral Service was particularly good his family and friends speak about him. Then we left for the cemetery, it was real and hard. I can't believe that I had to bury my father that day. My brother and his wife did an excellent job taking care of the funeral Service. My sister Marlene was with me for the funeral. We spent about six days in Trinidad, it was sad and fun at the same time. Now my father is resting in heaven. I love and miss you dad.

MY DAUGHTER AND SON

My daughter and son are the two most important people in my life. I also have four beautiful grandchildren. My kids are always checking up on me telling me mom to stop shopping, do not work too hard. But you know me I still go shopping and I still work a lot of overtime you cannot stop june the sweet prune I believe when your kids see you working hard, they will follow you. My kids call almost every day hi mom what are you doing. Did you eat. My daughter will surprise me with my favorite soup and smoothie, and my son will get me salad. I love eating salad almost every day and smoothies too. I think it will be nice if my grandkids come over and clean my house every week, I could bake them cake and cookies for their challenging work. We go to a lot of restaurants, especially all you can eat. We have a lot of fun for the family every time I am off, we go out if it's not a restaurant it the movies. When they were kids, I would take them to the zoo. Most important family come first. The grandkids always call me grandma, come over and take me to gallery painting show and the little one loves going to the store. On my way get dressed love you be outside in ten minutes.

TRAVELING

I love traveling when I grew up in Trinidad, I travel to the other Caribbeans Islands Like Barbados, Margarita ,Grenada, and Haiti. The most beautiful Islands you can visit. The water is sometimes blue and warm, I could stay in the water for hours. The people are friendly, the food is good, and the beach is even beautiful. My dream is to travel to more beautiful Countries. Tobago is the sister Island of Trinidad. Every month I travel there with my best friend. The beach is beautiful and has not gone there in twenty years. Every time I have more than three days off, I book a ticket and pack my suite case and go off to the airport for just a short vacation. It is fun to meet people when you are on vacation. I met a couple in Margarita, and I become close friends with them and become godmother to their son I was very happy that I was asked to be someone godmother and I went back, and I have a god son it was beautiful day meet a lot of people and I didn't even speak Spanish good. But I understand a little. My next trip will be to England and Paris some of my friend's that never Travel before afraid to go on a plane or ship not me I am going. Sometimes you can take a bus or train and just enjoy the ride, Sigh seeing meet new people enjoy the view. Best thing about traveling you meet people especially on cruise ship almost everyone asks where you from I didn't even know people was from all different Countries on the ship with me. The best thing is the entertainment and friendly people. I also love saving different currency from other countries. My favorite things to do on the ship are bingo and dancing. I love being available for myself it especially Important when I have the time I am going to travel.

I hope to have a family reunion on a cruise ship for like a four day eat and drink all day and talk about old times. I believe keeping up with memories and asking questions is especially important in the family. Or I would like to take my family to England or Paris that should be a lot of fun I know we're going to have a good time A few years ago my family all meet up in Florida and it was fun we spent four days on a cruise and three days black in Florida we went sightseeing ,amusement parks the best vacation ever.

DON'T COOK

Frist of all I do not like to cook. Growing up at my grandmother's house we had two house cleaners, so I never learned to cook. My mother never had us in the kitchen all we do was play, watch tv and homework. I also never teach my kids to, but they are particularly good cooks. I went to two cooking schools in Trinidad and New York and still do not cook. The truth is when I cook my food does not taste right. That is one of the reasons I don't like cooking but once a week is good. I will take my time and do my best. But I also like going to the restaurant once or twice a week. or I will pick up something to go I am willing to change and start cooking at home. I love eating out, especially getting my salad, smoothies, and milkshakes is something I am not giving up. I have eaten out for years and I know I am getting older I am willing to change. Eating healthy is important so I am going to get some cookbooks and do more cooking at home. When I want to have something special to eat, I will just get in my car and drive to my favorite restaurant, that is what makes me happy eating out.

WENT TO EMERGENCY ROOM

I had pain in my knee and right ankle for months. One day on my way to work I could not open the door at work. I tried to clock in. I could not reach the clock machine to swipe in. I was in so much pain when I finally clock in went to floor my supervisor asked me what is wrong is ok, and I told her I cannot move I am in so much pain. My supervisor got me a wheelchair and took me to the Emergency Room. I had an MRI and the doctor told me that I had tears in my knee and fluid in my ankle that year I had two surgeries. My ankle and my left knee and the next year one more so three surgeries in eight months. Out of work for three months and was in pain every day. It was not easy but that is my everyday life. Was in pain day and night, the medicine was not working, people say it takes about a year to heal and therapy will help. I had no choice but to take a pain pill for the pain when I got up in the morning. At work on my feet all day I was in pain. I could not even go to the Supermarket walking was hard when I could not take it no more I decided to make appointment with my doctor for the Injections the first one was good I got the Injections at three pm when I left the Doctor office I went to the Supermarket and also did my laundry I even cut the grass at seven pm the pain came back I could not walk my biggest mistake was not going home and getting some rest I decide to have more Injection and they did not work I had no choice but to get my knee replacement on my left knee.

SURGERY

I cannot believe in the next twenty-four hours I'll be getting surgery again. My son is on his way to take me for my surgery and cannot wait for this Knee replacement surgery to be over. I am home in bed resting. The pain meds did not work. I called the doctor and asked for medicine, nothing works still in pain day and night Home for three months and a lot of therapy. Cannot wait to go back to work and the pain to be over. Knee replacement is not easy, it's painful every day. My doctor says I will have pain for a year and may still have pain for some time . It has been over three months now, still in pain back to work twelve-hour shift and waiting for the year to over to see if this knee surgery really works. when you have surgery a lot of things you can do, I was not allowed to drive for two weeks but I drive the first week I had therapy every other day.my grandson help me he brings my food and ice, tea and snacks. In bed all day watching TV, reading magazines, but I made it through my surgery. After two months I felt a little better so I when to the movies and did some shopping. I had fun days visiting friends and spent about four days in New York. My first day back at work was hectic. I was walking in pain, I had to take my medication twice a day, it was not easy. My coworkers were an immense help and always assisted me and asking june are you ok. I did miss everyone, and I was so happy to be back at work. But pain or no pain I will be doing overtime making that money

WINE

I love drinking wine. one of my favorite things to do after work is going to the bar with my coworkers and have fun. I sometimes go with my friends or alone. The best thing is I can call my friends hi meet me at the bar. But sitting at home watching Television or listing to music with a glass of wine is the best relaxing moment. And good therapy for my soul, mind, body after a hard day's work. In my bedroom I have over twenty-one bottles of wine and some more in other rooms love drinking wine. For my birthday and Christmas everybody knows what I want wine and more wine. My hobby is collecting bottles of wine from all different countries. A glass of wine before I go to sleep is the best way to get a good night's sleep. I remember when my grandfather came home with big bottles of wine, I was amazed at the bottles design. My father only bye wine for Christmas. I love giving wine as gifts. I believe most of my friends like my gift. When I am in New York I will go to my mother's house and across the street there is a liquor store and the first thing I do is go over and get some for my friends. When they come over, we will have fun wine and some tasty food they can't past that up. I went on a cruise a few years ago and on the cruise the prices of the wine were reasonable, and I had fun. It was one of my favorite times. The ship had all kinds of liquor, and you can drink all day. When I was living in Trinidad on a weekend my friends invited me to play pool, I believe that is when I start drinking wine. And I love it to this day. I also go to the liquor store when there a sale and look at different new wine I guess it is a hobby I will not give up.

MOTHER

My mother a strong hard-working woman takes no nonsense like to travel she travel to Puerto Rico, England and visit Las Vegas. we went on a cruise to Bahamas it was beautiful four days and three nights we went every attraction on the cruise the food was good. I had wine and pina colada all day. My mother was eating nonstop. I say do you know we are having dinner soon. Arrive in the Bahamas spend the entire day we had coconut water and cake, bought souvenirs, and a little elephant made out of wood. Even got some Bahamian coconut rum spent a few hours taking pictures and sightseeing watching the dolphins. We had the best tour guide in the Bahamas. Back in Florida went to movies and restaurants, did some shopping, I had an enjoyable time with my mother. This woman also like gambling she go to the casino three to four times a year. Do not disturb her when her favorite wresting show is on TV. Love to cook oxtail rice and peas, fry bake and fry fist. A busy woman always on the go. play mask when she was younger, and the center of the party loves to dance.

MORNING

First thing in the morning, I say my prayers, get my clothes ready and ironed for work, take a shower, comb my hair, do my makeup, word of advice is to never leave the house without saying your prayers. I always like to start my car up for a couple minutes to warm up the engine and to heat up the windshield because during the fall and winter the windshield is very foggy and difficult to see through .Every morning I stop for my lottery tickets and favorite smoothie beverage to start my day off right and in a good mindset , which is my absolute everyday happiness. I also look outside and see if the sun is out, play with my puppy for five to ten minutes. Now it is time to get ready for work, see you later. On my way to work I listen to music on my favorite radio stations in my local area. When I arrive, I stay in the parking lot and have my bread fast in the car. Relax for ten minutes and I am ready for work. Being at work does not feel like work sometimes because have over twenty-Eight years in the medical field and I love it. I think I am more at work done home. My first day at work was the day my grandson Steve was born . And I could not miss the first day of work. After work I visited my handsome grandson. That is the day I will always remember the start of my new job and still working hard. I love my job getting up every morning and going to work.

MY DOG

My lovable puppy was born in February 2006. He is an incredibly special dog. When he wants his snacks, he will go outside and come back inside for his snacks. Also, very protective of me, he will bark at anyone who gets too close to me but once they give him a treat, he becomes too nice and cute. He also loves to sleep in his special room, and he likes to sleep and play in my bedroom. He is the love of my life. When I'm home he only wants my attention, my grandson is home with pocklerlips barks a lot but when I'm not home he lovable to him I believe dogs are smarter than we think, he eats at a special time when I come home he's right by the front door waiting for me to pick him up he love to cuddle If he don't like the taste his snacks or food he will not eat and also don't like to brushed his teeth and sometimes staying all day without eating his food he will wait until I come home. He is a beautiful dog who loves playing in the backyard. If he could talk pocklerlips would say one hot sunny day I decided to trick Stevie. He let me outside pee, and I was smelling the sweet flowers and noticed the buzzing and bees eating the yellow flowers. I was curious and wanted to see what the hype was about, so I ate the grass and flowers and yes it did not go so well. I went inside to lay down. I did not care about the cookie, my stomach was hurting, and I threw up green slime, let us just say I was caught red handed because Stevie was watching out the window. If my dog could talk to me.

LUNA

Luna is a sweet cat. She is gray with black stripes and big green eyes. She comes to my house every week. She was about 5 months when she was adopted. She loves to eat her cat food and dog food. She loves to sleep all day and watch the birds outside the window. She enjoys playing with her toys, especially ones with feathers. Luna also likes to watch Ginny, the dog, but fears her. She has two places where she can sleep but likes to sleep in human beds instead. One day, we found out that Luna had fleas and were surprised because she is an indoor cat and did not know how she got fleas. We bought a special shampoo to wash her, and she was NOT happy. When the water touched her, she began to jump out of the tub and run to the door. We brushed her every day for a week and eventually the fleas went away. Luna loves her home, and she hates it when she goes to unfamiliar places. When Luna went to June's house for the first time she hid under a bed for a whole week. Luna is trained to sit, spin, give nose kisses and lay down.

GINNY

Ginny was adopted on March 15, 2022. She is a beautiful Husky with one brown eye and another half brown and half white. Everyone loves her eyes and people are always saying how pretty she is. Ginny loves to go on walks, eat human food, play with her toys and go to the dog park. When she goes to the dog park, she likes people more than dogs. She plays withs dogs for 2 minutes and then spends an hour getting petted by people. When people are eating, she lays down under the table, waiting for food to fall on the floor so she can eat it. Ginny loves to sniff trees, grass and rocks when she goes on walks. Ginny has her own dog bed, but she loves to lay down on the sofa. She barks every time the mail man comes drop off mail. Ginny loves it when people visit and is very friendly with everyone. She does not bark a lot, but she will howl when she wants human food or protecting someone. Ginny is trained to sit, lay down, give her paw, come and stay.

MY SON & HIS FIANCÉE

Chris met Karina in November of 2018. They went on their first trip together in July 2019, to California. They walked to the Hollywood sign in 90-degree weather and took a lot of photos. Chris favorite thing to do in California was watching the sunset at Sunset cliff and kayaking. Karina's mom lives in Washinton state, and they visit whenever they can. The first time it was very cold, and Chris did not like it. The second time, the weather was better, and they hiked to see Mt. Rainer. Karina is from Mexico and Chris's parents are from Haiti and Trinidad. They both like to eat each other's nationality food. Karina likes to eat rice and beans with Griot. Chris likes to eat Tacos with red salsa from a food truck near their house. When they are not working, they like to watch funny movies and cooking shows. Chris likes to play video games and Karina likes to collect Starbucks cups. Karina only has one brother, and they are 10 years apart, almost like Chris and his sister.

STAY IN MY BED LATE

I stay in my bed late sometimes my puppy barks and wakes me up to take him outside when he comes back inside, I will go right back to bed when I finally decide to get up, I do my laundry, vacuum and make breakfast. After that head for the store and take a walk in the mall and go to the movies. On my way home stop at the supermarket to spend money and buy things that I do not need, which is what I do all the time. Pick up a smoothie and sometimes I get my grandkids their favorite smoothies. On my day off love going to New York and Atlantic City. Spending time at home is also fun if you do not feel like going out. I just spend all day in my bed watching TV and ordering food, sometimes milkshake love my milkshake. Make time and call family and friends say hi people hope all is well . A cup of hot coffee, my favorite in the morning by the fire. My grandkids come over and we bake cookies and make cake. My home-made cake is full of fruits. With the help of my late grandmother Helena joseph recipes, she can bake. I remember making old fashioned cupcakes and coconut sweet cake. She also bakes bread every weekend and my favorite sweet bread; I love going to the restaurant to get my self-number one order pina colada .Cooking is not my thing, but I do it sometimes. I believe when you have a day off you should enjoy it to the best. Being available for yourself is especially important. Happy hour is always my favorite. You get more for your money so Going once or twice a week to have an enjoyable time with friends and family is good to enjoy the food and the wine. Trying different restaurants is my favorite thing to do, especially when it is my day off. I will try a new restaurant the smell of the food and the taste is so good. Even the bakery fresh bread and cakes I will say please can you wrap up this cake I would like to take is for my friends, walking down the street I saw this beautiful big flea market, and in this flea, market had some old cookbooks and I bought about five. They were cheap. I had to get them. I also got some for my mother, sister and daughter. What a day off when I get back home, I will be cooking with my family and eating right which is especially important.

MY SWEET PRUNE GRANDCHILDREN

My four grandchildren are a piece of work, but I love them so much. My daughter, Natalie, had a son named Nyron on September 6th, so I wound up becoming a grandma. Nyron is my only grandson who is so funny and always knows how to make me laugh. He is working on studying to begin a career in health care. Although, he must always wear long sleeve shirts because he decided to put tattoos covering his entire upper body. My first granddaughter was Najee that loves basketball. Every day she travels somewhere for practice, training or a game to play the sport and she was granted a commitment to Rutgers University. Najee was not only great at sports, but she was academically sound in the classroom gaining so many awards and scholarships. Now, she is also studying to become a doctor in medicine. Nejaa was the next granddaughter that came a year after Najee; she was more creative than athletic. Just like her grandma she ended up being left-handed. She is so smart with her schooling that she always gets straight "A" grades. She has been a manager for a major corporation for years and is also in college studying medicine. Her favorite task is ordering fast food from a different restaurant every day. Lucky was the dog that Nejaa wanted for her birthday, so he is part of the family, too. He is a handful and his favorite thing to do is bark at random people all day long. Lastly, Nalle was born in June she is the youngest grandchild She is doing great with her schoolwork and meeting new friends. Her favorite hobby is freely painting portraits with calming music. Do not forget she loves to spend money on food and clothes. All the girls are smarty pants as they were all inducted into their school's National Honors Society.